SpongeBob SquarePants

IN A FIX

S0-BYX-582

by Sonia Sander

SCHOLASTIC INC.

New York   Toronto   London   Auckland   Sydney
Mexico City   New Delhi   Hong Kong   Buenos Aires

"What is this big thing in your sink?" asked SpongeBob.

"It is a strainer," said Squidward.

"Feel free to borrow it and leave."

"This is great for jellyfishing!" said Patrick.

"It was nice of Squidward to let us use it," said SpongeBob.

Patrick slipped,
then tripped.
He missed the jellyfish
and hit the ground.

"Hopping clams! It ripped a bit!" said SpongeBob. "How can we fix it?" asked Patrick.

"We will fix it with a hammer," said SpongeBob. "We will hit it just like this."

"We did not catch any jellyfish, but it was nice of you to let us use this," Patrick told Squidward.

"How did you fix it?"
  asked Squidward.
"I gave it to you broken."
"Oh, it was no big deal,"
  said SpongeBob.
"We are good at fixing
  things."

"Hey, Squidward," cried SpongeBob. "We will fix up your whole house if you want!"